GOOD ROSIE!

KATE DiCAMILLO

PICTURES BY
HARRY BLISS

CANDLEWICK PRESS

First edition 2018

Library of Congress Catalog Card Number pending
ISBN 978-0-7636-8979-7

18 19 20 21 22 23 APS 10 9 8 7 6 5 4 3 2 1

Printed in Humen, Dongguan, China

This book was typeset in Myriad Pro.
The illustrations were done in watercolor.

Candlewick Press
99 Dover Street
Somerville, Massachusetts 02144

visit us at www.candlewick.com

For Ramona
and for Remy, Hazel, Louie, Agatha, Poppy, and Fred
and for Henry, of course
K. D.

For Sofi, my beautiful muse
H. B.

Rosie lives with George.
Rosie is a good dog.

Every morning, Rosie and George eat breakfast together. George has two poached eggs. Rosie eats kibble from a big silver bowl.

When the bowl is empty, Rosie can see another dog staring back at her.

"Hello!" says Rosie.

Ruff!

Rosie and George walk together.

Sometimes, Rosie chases squirrels.
She runs very fast, as fast as she can.
But she never catches anything.

Rosie, get back here!

Rosie always returns to George.

Good, Rosie. Good dog.

George thinks that most clouds look like presidents.
Rosie thinks that most clouds look like squirrels.

One day, George sees something different in the clouds.

Look, Rosie!
That one looks
like a dog!

The cloud *does* look like a dog!
Rosie wags her tail.
"Hello, hello!" she shouts.

Woof, woof!

The dog cloud does not answer her.
Rosie feels lonely in an
empty-silver-bowl sort of way.

Something new is the dog park.

Rosie does not like the dog park.
There are too many dogs.
She doesn't know any of them.

It makes Rosie feel lonely to look at
so many strange dogs.

"My name is, uh, Maurice," says a very big dog. "And I have a bunny."

Rosie growls.

GRRRRrrrr . . .

Rosie is not a bad dog.
She is a good dog.
But she can't help it.
She doesn't like Maurice.
Or his bunny.

grrr . . .

Maurice shakes his stuffed bunny.
He shakes it very, very hard.

He drops the bunny on the ground.
Maurice says, "Wanna, uh, play bunny?"

"I want to go home,"
Rosie says to George.

Woof!

But something is bouncing toward Rosie.
The something is a very small dog with a very sparkly collar.

"I'm Fifi! I'm Fifi!" says the small dog.
"It says *Fifi* right on my collar! See?
My name is spelled out in shiny stones.
What's your name?"

"Uh," Maurice says to Fifi,
"do *you* want to play?"

"Me?" says Fifi.

Maurice wags his tail.

Maurice crouches.

Maurice pounces.

Maurice picks up Fifi and
shakes her like a stuffed bunny!

Fifi is in trouble!
Somebody has to do something!

Somebody is Rosie.

"Ouch," says Maurice. He opens his mouth.
Fifi falls to the ground with a small thud.

Fifi says, "Am I alive?"
Rosie says, "Yes."

Fifi stands up. She wags her tail.

Her collar sparkles.
Her legs tremble.
She holds her tiny head up high
and says, "I'm Fifi and I'm alive!"

For the first time, Rosie likes Fifi.
Just a little bit.

Maurice coughs. He says, "Uh, gee."

He spits three tiny stones onto the ground.

Rosie closes her eyes.
She thinks about her empty bowl.
She opens her eyes and looks up at the clouds in the sky.
"I don't know," says Rosie. "I'm not sure how you do it."

"Do you want to be friends with a dog named Fif?" Fif says to Rosie.

"I do," says Rosie. She is surprised to hear herself say it. "I do want to be friends with a dog named Fif."

"*That's* how you make friends," says Fif to Maurice.

Maurice says, "Uh, okay, would you be friends with a dog named Maurice? If he — uh, let's see — if he promised not to swallow any more of your tiny shiny things?"

Rosie wants to stay.

In the morning, George eats two poached eggs. Rosie eats kibble out of her silver bowl.

When breakfast is over, George says,

Dog park, Rosie?

And Rosie walks away from her bowl without looking back.

At the dog park, Fif is waiting.
Maurice is waiting, too.

"Come on, Fif! Come on, Maurice!
Let's play!" says Rosie.

Rosie chases Fif.

They run very fast.

Maurice chases Rosie.

Sometimes, they catch each other.